Olly Jolly Says

COUNT YOUR BLESSINGS

by

Sundari Francis-Bala

Illustrated by Penny Margolis

Published by:

FriesenPress

Suite 300 — 852 Fort Street
Victoria, BC, Canada V8W 1H8

www.friesenpress.com

Distributed to the trade by The Ingram Book Company

Acknowledgements

I am deeply appreciative of:

the first impetus to self-publish and the professional advice provided by Tim Lindsay of FriesenPress at the start of this project,

the exceptional guidance and dedication provided by Caroline Shaw, my author account manager at FriesenPress, during the process,

the many loving hours poured into the artistic realization of this story by Al and Penny Margolis,

the artistic concept for Olly Jolly suggested by Priya Bala-Miller and the editorial support given by Blair Miller, and

the reviews and encouragement generously offered by many good friends : they know who they are.

Dedication

For my children, Siddhartha, Priya and Sudeep and my
grandchildren, Miles and Graham

You may have read the fairy tale of the princess who never smiled until she saw a funny sight. Well, this is a similar story of Boy, who lived with his parents in a city like yours.

He had loving parents, a small, but comfortable and clean house, nice clothes and shoes to wear, and a few cool toys to play with.

At school, Boy had many friends and he enjoyed learning from his teachers. (Once, he even got a special award for storytelling!) In short, he had everything to make him a satisfied little boy.

So, nobody knew why Boy always had a sad look on his face, and you cannot blame him because he himself didn't know this! (However, if you looked at his yearbook pictures, you could see that all the children except Boy would be smiling!)

The one thing Boy really liked to do was to read books. He loved to read the fairy tales in the book his father gave him for his fifth birthday, the stories of adventure, the myths and the legends of faraway countries, the comics, and sometimes, even bills and bits of newspapers.

Very often, as Boy read, he would dream of wonderful lands like Norway, where the sun shone even at midnight in the summer, magical people like the shamans in Peru, quaint trees like the baobab in Africa, laughing birds like the kookaburra in Australia, and the flowers that bloomed once in twelve years and gave the colour to the Blue Mountains in India.

One night, as he was getting ready to sleep and reading from his picture book, he had a far-away look in his eyes.

He imagined camels flying over the pyramids of Egypt on their way to the Emperor's Palace in China.

Suddenly, he heard a little low voice beside him, "Why do you have a faraway look in your eyes, Boy?"

Boy was startled, because there — in front of him — was the helpful, magical bee, Olly Jolly. How did she get out of his picture book, Boy wondered.

"Who are you?" he asked, unable to hide the surprise in his voice, even though he recognized her. "You can't be real!" he said, and his eyes grew wide.

"I am very real. Pinch yourself if you think you are still dreaming!", Olly Jolly said, whizzing and flying around the room like a tornado! "All my friends talk about you as the boy who never smiles and they've sent me to find out why!"

"... and find out, I must," she thought to herself.

Boy was glad to have some company. "I just don't know why I don't feel good sometimes", Boy sighed.

"Well, it's OK to feel sad sometimes, you know, but would you like me to tell you what *I* do to make myself feel better?" asked Olly Jolly ever so gently.

"Oh yes... please do tell me," Boy said eagerly, and thinking she might have some magic.

"It's very simple, really," Olly Jolly said, sitting cross-legged on the bed, and making herself more comfortable. "I just start counting my special blessings."

"But I don't have any special blessings!" replied Boy frowning rather sadly.

"That's not so," Olly Jolly quickly replied, wagging her finger and speaking in a singsong way, flying around so that Boy had to turn his head this way and that way really quickly to keep up with her.

"All of us have blessings, Boy, if we only care to count them."

"Just close your eyes and think of all the colors you can see," Olly Jolly suggested, still singing. Boy obediently closed his eyes. In his mind, he could see the colours of a summer garden— orange and blue and purple and yellow— and it made him feel warm and nice inside.

Still with his eyes closed, he heard Olly Jolly continue to sing slowly:

"Imagine, Boy, imagine —
the sound of the running stream,
the lilies you can smell in your garden,
the rain in the summer,
and the sunshine in the winter,
the morning freshness ...

13

"and the lacy spider web with frost on your window! Isn't that a pretty sight, now?

How about the moon and stars on a clear blue night, especially the stars that form shapes in the sky...?"

Olly Jolly continued to sing, "the old forests and the pure waterfalls deep inside them, the rivers that wind through mountains and valleys till they reach the sea — aren't they blessings?"

"Yes, I suppose so," Boy replied, enjoying all the pictures he was creating in his mind.

"Then, can you count the people who love you — your family and friends — aren't they blessings?" Olly Jolly quizzed.

"Yes, I do think my mommy and daddy love me very much, even though they give me *Time Out* sometimes," Boy said, beginning to feel a bit differently.

"And how about the fine school you go to... and Smokey, your pet dog?"

Boy was already thinking of all his other blessings; and when Olly Jolly said, "Blessings are rainbows,"

Boy added, "the present from my uncle (he remembered now, for it came in a rainbow-colored gift bag),

the invitation to my friend Marvic's birthday party tomorrow,

the smile on my baby sister's face,

the sea shells that I collected for my school project,

my new teacher...

As he was counting his blessings, he saw Olly Jolly flying away...

"Oh, please don't go away yet!" Boy cried out, but Olly Jolly only smiled sweetly and waved, as she said, "just keep going...keep on counting your blessings and you'll be fine... and keep smiling".

From that time onwards, whenever Boy didn't feel so good, he would remember his friend Olly Jolly and begin counting his blessings. As he realized he had so many of them, you can be sure he became a happy, cheerful boy, always smiling as he wondered how he came to have so many wonderful blessings.

My List of Blessings

Draw some of your blessings or use pictures
and photographs.

About the Author

Coming from a military family that lived all over India, Sundari Francis-Bala has been enchanted with the mystery of the unknown since childhood. Her love of the English Language led her to pursue degrees in British and American Literature, and a PhD in Post-Colonial Commonwealth Literature. She enjoyed a fulfilling 41-year career teaching English at post-secondary institutions in Bangalore, Dubai, and Vancouver.

Sundari is blessed with three inspiring children and two grandchildren, who, to her delight, live near the Catskill Mountains, the setting for Rip Van Winkle, one of her favourite childhood stories. Sundari's eclectic interests range from experiments in the kitchen and garden, to history and cinema. She funds a "goat project" for education in rural India and sponsors a child through World Vision. 50% of the profits from this book will go towards meeting the educational needs of children in India and Canada.